Noni the Blacksmith

by Catherine Farnell

illustrated by Lucy Richards

This book has been produced as part of the Blackdowns Metal Makers project by The Carousel Project with the kind support of our funders:

The Heritage Lottery Fund

Blackdown Hills Area of Outstanding Natural Beauty (AONB) Partnership

Special thanks to:

The Blackdown Hills AONB team

Hemyock Preschool and Primary School

Zoe Kenyon (story editor)

The Blackdown Hills AONB, on the border of Devon and Somerset, is a very special place with a unique iron working heritage. We hope that this book will help a younger audience to find out more about it.

The rights of Catherine Farnell to be identified as the Author of the work have been as asserted by her in accordance with the Copyright, Designs and Patents Act 1988.

A catalogue record for this book is available on request from the British Library.

OTCEditions

Noni was a girl who lived on the
Blackdown Hills, near Dumpdon
Hill Fort, more than 2,000 years
ago in a time called the Iron Age....

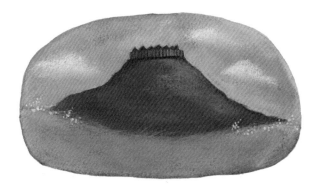

Noni had a lot of wishes. She wished she could fly as high as a bird, run as fast as a deer and grow as tall as a tree. But most of all, she wished she could be a blacksmith, just like her Daddy.

She watched him use the magic of fire to turn special stones into swords and shields and knives, and she knew she wanted to do the same.

On Noni's birthday, her Daddy made her a beautiful iron knife. It felt smooth and hard. It glinted in the sunlight.

He told her to keep it safe.

'If you look after this knife very carefully, when you are grown up I will show you how to make one all by yourself,' he said.

Noni loved her knife, but she loved the idea of making her own even more.

'Can't you show me now?' she said.
'No, Noni. You're too young.' Her Daddy shook his head.

'Too young? I'm not too young!' Noni stamped her feet. She thought her Daddy was wrong.

Noni knew that her Daddy collected clay, special stones and wood from the other side of the hill fort. She decided that she would show she was not too young to be a blacksmith by finding these things herself.

Noni set off with her pony Dum Dum. Her precious knife was tied around her waist. It was a long way, but Noni didn't feel tired.

We're going on an iron hunt
Dum Dum and me
Over the hill for iron ore
Then wood from the trees
Last to the river
To find some clay
I'm going to be a blacksmith
I start today!

First, Noni dug for iron ore in the hard ground. She placed the special stones in the bags on one side of Dum Dum's back. Next, she collected wood from the dark forest. She tied this to the other side of Dum Dum's back.

Finally, they headed for the big river.

Noni waded into the river. She searched for clay under the cold water, filling her leather bag with what she found.

She was so busy that she didn't notice her knife slip into the water with a splash.

When she had collected as much clay as Dum Dum could carry, Noni turned for home. She felt for her knife, but it had gone.

'Where is my precious knife?' she cried.

She searched and searched, but the river had carried it away
and it was nowhere to be found.

Noni sat on the riverbank.
Tears fell down her cheeks
and on to her tunic.

'What shall I do?' she asked Dum Dum. 'Now I have lost my knife, Daddy will never show me how to be a blacksmith.' Dum Dum blew on her long hair and Noni cried even harder.

It wasn't until the sun began to set that they headed home. Noni knew that her Daddy would be very cross.

Noni and Dum Dum trudged up the side of the steep hill fort, across the top and down the other side.

She could just make out their village. Its small fires glowed a welcome in the dark.

Noni's Daddy rushed out of their roundhouse.

'Where have you been?' he shouted. 'It is dark. I have been so worried!'

'I'm sorry,' said Noni. Tears fell from her eyes again. 'I'm so sorry, Daddy. I lost my knife.'

She explained how she had gone in search of clay, iron ore and wood to prove that she could be a blacksmith. When he saw the heavy load that Dum Dum was carrying, her Daddy knew that Noni was ready to learn.

'I am sad that you lost your knife, Noni. But I am very happy that you are back safe and sound,' he said. 'Now let's get to work.'

Together, the two of them made Noni a brand new knife.

They used the clay that Noni had collected to repair the furnace. They used her wood to make a fire. They smelted the iron ore from the stones in the heat of the flames. They heated and beat the precious iron bloom that came out of the furnace.

They heated and beat it, heated and beat it into the shape of a knife.

Heat, heat, heat, red hot!
Beat, beat, beat, beat!

Heat, heat, heat, red hot!
Beat, beat, beat, beat!

Until the knife is done!

Noni's Daddy hugged her.

'What a fine knife you have made,' he said.

Noni was proud of the knife but, most of all, she was proud to know that one day she would be a blacksmith, just like her Daddy....

Noni's Song

(sing to the tune of 'Row, Row, Row Your Boat')

Noni was a little girl
From the Iron Age
Her Daddy was a blacksmith
She longed to be the same

Noni went with Dum Dum
On a long journey
Wanted clay, wood, iron ore
To prove that she was ready

She knows to dig for iron ore
Finds wood beneath the trees
Clay from the water
Everything she needs

Noni lost her special knife
She was very sad
Her Daddy could not be cross
Her work had made him glad

Clay to build the furnace
Wood to stoke the fire
Iron bloom smelted out
Ready for the hammer

Noni was so happy now
A blacksmith she became
Just like her Daddy
They were now the same

Noni's Journey

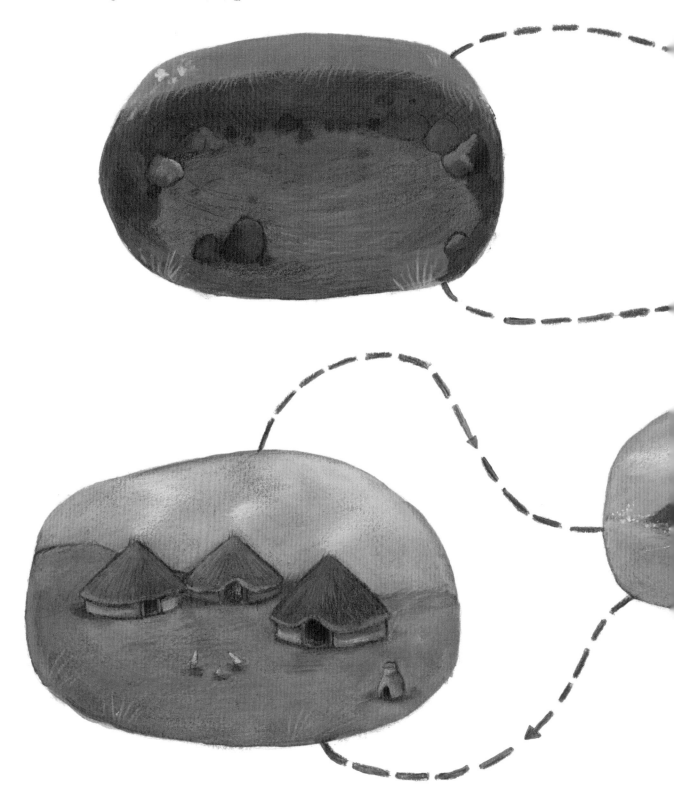

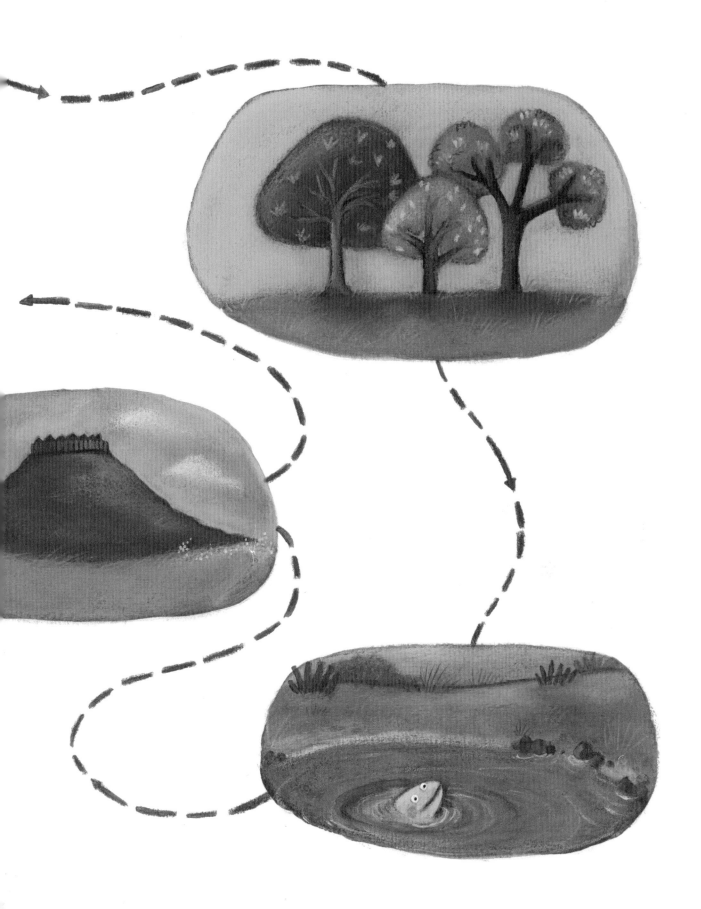

Noni saw lots of interesting plants and animals on her journey.
Did you see them too?

JAY

DRAGONFLY

MISTLE THRUSH

HARE

OTTER

Why did Noni need these things?

IRON ORE

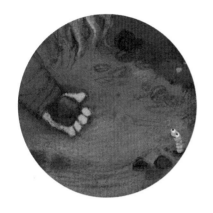

CLAY AND WOOD

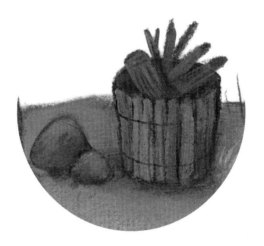

FURNACE

To find out more about Noni's world, explore Blackdowns Metal Makers at
www.blackdownhillsaonb.org.uk.

You can view and listen to the story online, hear the songs, watch fun videos
and download a family friendly guide to places to visit.

There are also resources for adults who want to learn more about ancient iron working
in the Blackdown Hills.

The three songs and rhymes in this story were written by musician Emily Davey
with children from Hemyock Preschool and Primary School.

Find out more about early years arts and creative learning initiative
The Carousel Project by visiting www.thecarouselproject.org.uk.